SHAWNEE BILL'S
ENCHANTED FIVE-RIDE
❖ CARROUSEL ❖

SHAWNEE BILL'S
ENCHANTED FIVE-RIDE
CARROUSEL

BY COOPER EDENS
ILLUSTRATED BY DANIEL LANE

GREEN TIGER PRESS

PUBLISHED BY SIMON & SCHUSTER
NEW YORK • LONDON • TORONTO • SYDNEY • TOKYO • SINGAPORE

Every Fourth of July, the town of North Valley holds a carnival. There are fireworks, a swing band, a sideshow, delicious food, and free rides of all kinds.

The children's favorite is Shawnee Bill's Enchanted Five-Ride Carrousel with its beautiful black swan, glorious green tiger, burly brown bear, galloping gold pony, and its whimsical white rabbit.

STRONG MAN

Around midnight, after the carnival has closed down, Shawnee Bill hitches up his trailer and heads out of town. But don't think the night is over for Shawnee Bill or his animals.

Shawnee Bill, you see, has not
forgotten the babes, too young to come
to the carnival, who have been asleep
in their cribs while their older sisters
and brothers have been riding on his
wonderful carrousel.

Once out of town, Shawnee Bill parks on the old stone bridge
and, with a wink and a whistle, sets his carrousel animals free.

They go quietly to the sleeping babes, gently wake them,
and invite them into the moonlight.

As the sun rises, the animals return the babes safely to their cribs.
Then they return to Shawnee Bill, who glows with delight,
having heard the laughter of the babes carried on the night wind.

Then, off they go to their secret hideaway, not to be seen again until the next Fourth of July.

Except, of course, in children's dreams.

To Mony on a pony…

—C.E.

For Walt and Mary
and special thanks to Len Rose

—D.L.

GREEN TIGER PRESS
Simon & Schuster Building, Rockefeller Center
1230 Avenue of the Americas, New York, New York, 10020
Text copyright © 1994 by Cooper Edens
Illustrations copyright © 1994 by Daniel Lane
All rights reserved including the right of reproduction
in whole or in part in any form.
GREEN TIGER PRESS is an imprint of Simon & Schuster.
Typography by Sylvia Frezzolini
Manufactured in the United States of America

10 9 8 7 6 5 4 3 2 1

Library of Congress Cataloging-in-Publication Data
Edens, Cooper.   Shawnee Bill's enchanted five-ride carrousel / by
Cooper Edens ; illustrated by Daniel Lane.   p.   cm.   Summary: Every
summer at the North Valley carnival, after they have spent the day
giving rides to the older children, the animals of Shawnee Bill's
Enchanted Five-Ride Carrousel come to life in the darkness and bring
delight to the babes who are home in their cribs and thus missed the fun.
[1. Merry-go-round—Fiction. 2. Carnivals—Fiction. 3. Animals—
Fiction.] I. Lane, Daniel, ill. II. Title.
PZ7.E223Sh 1994 91-30135
[E]—dc20 CIP
ISBN: 0-671-75952-3

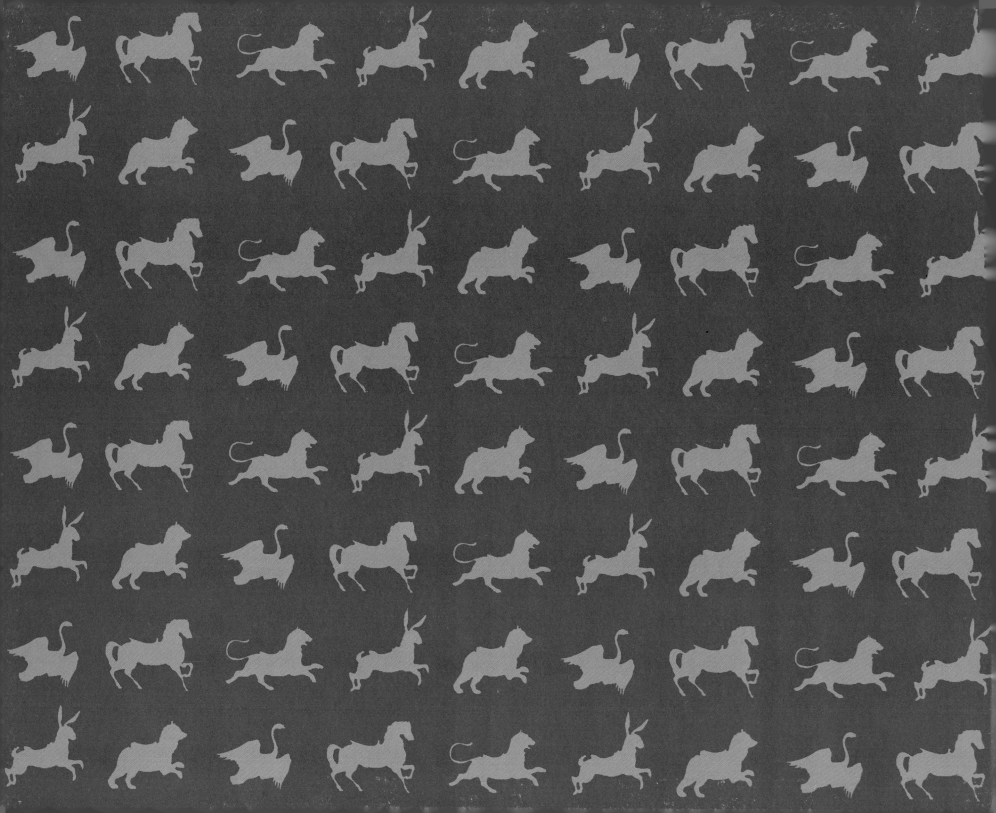